God is light,

and in Him

is no darkness

at all.

1 JOHN 1:5

The Lightlings

WRITTEN BY

R.C. Sproul

ILLUSTRATED BY

Justin Gerard

ℝ

Reformation Trust

A DIVISION OF LIGONIER MINISTRIES · ORLANDO, FLORIDA

To beloved grandchildren:
Darby, Campbell, Shannon, Delaney,
Erin Claire, Maili, and Reilly.

-R.C. Sproul

ONE EVENING, in a house in a quiet neighborhood, a little boy was getting ready for bed. The boy's name was Charlie Cobb. As his mother was tucking him in, she covered him with blankets to make him warm and cozy. She knelt by his bed and prayed with him. Then she stood, leaned over, and kissed his forehead.

Charlie looked up at her and said, "Mommy, please don't forget to turn on the night light before you leave my room." Mrs. Cobb smiled at him and said, "Don't worry, Sweetheart. I'll be sure to turn on the light. I won't leave you in the dark."

So Charlie's mother gave him one last kiss, finished tucking him in, and turned on the night light next to his bed. Just as she was ready to leave, Charlie said, "Mommy? Why am I afraid of the dark?"

She said, "That's a hard question to answer, Charlie. I think we're going to have to save that question for Grandpa. He's coming for dinner tomorrow. You can ask him then."

"All right, Mommy," Charlie said. "I'll wait until tomorrow and ask Grandpa about it."

The next day, just as Charlie's mother had promised, Grandpa came for dinner. Before they moved to the table, Charlie went and sat on Grandpa's knee and said, "Grandpa, may I ask you a question that's really bothering me?"

Grandpa smiled and said, "Of course, Charlie, tell me what you'd like to know."

Charlie said, "Grandpa, why am I afraid of the dark? And why do so many people I know seem to be afraid of the dark, too?"

Grandpa looked at Charlie and said, "That's a very good question. But you know, not only are lots of people afraid of the dark, many people are afraid of the light."

"Afraid of the light?" said Charlie. "Why would that be?"

Grandpa said, "To understand that, I have to start at the beginning – in fact, at the very beginning."

Charlie loved it when Grandpa told him stories. So he curled up next to Grandpa and waited for him to begin. Grandpa started his story the way he always did:

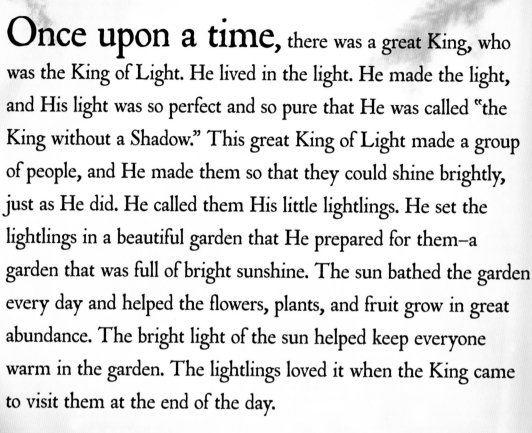

Once upon a time, there was a great King, who was the King of Light. He lived in the light. He made the light, and His light was so perfect and so pure that He was called "the King without a Shadow." This great King of Light made a group of people, and He made them so that they could shine brightly, just as He did. He called them His little lightlings. He set the lightlings in a beautiful garden that He prepared for them—a garden that was full of bright sunshine. The sun bathed the garden every day and helped the flowers, plants, and fruit grow in great abundance. The bright light of the sun helped keep everyone warm in the garden. The lightlings loved it when the King came to visit them at the end of the day.

But one day something terrible happened. The lightlings decided to do what they wanted to do instead of what their King commanded them to do. So they disobeyed the King and sinned against Him. The very moment they sinned, their lights became dim and they were filled with shame and great embarrassment. They ran as fast as they could to get away from the King. They didn't want the King of Light to see them. They ran out of the garden and into the woods, and hid themselves in the darkest place they could find. From then on, they were afraid of the light, because they knew that where the light was, the King would be, and the King would see them in their shame.

After the lightlings left, the King began to remove His light from the garden. It soon became cold and covered with weeds, thorns, and sticky briars. The lightlings moved further and further into the woods, until they lived in a place that was almost completely covered in darkness. It was so dark, they had to grope around as if they were blind, feeling their way through the forest. Often they would trip and fall, scuffing their knees and bruising themselves.

It was awful living in the dreadful darkness all the time, where the only light they ever saw was in barely lit shadows that danced in the forest. In fact, they couldn't tell the difference anymore between night and day.

Then one night, or perhaps it was day, far off in the distance they saw a blinding light shining through the trees. They could see the light coming from miles and miles away. They were frightened by it. They thought the light meant that the King was coming to find them to punish them for their sins. So most of the lightlings began to stumble quickly away from the light.

But some of the lightling children were so amazed by the light and curious about it that they decided to see from where it was coming. They set off and traveled for miles and miles. It took them a long time, but as they moved, they saw the light shining brighter and brighter.

Finally, they came to a clearing in the forest. In the middle of the clearing, they saw a father lightling, a mother lightling, and a baby who was shining like the sun. The blazing light seemed to be coming right out of the baby Himself.

The lightlings who saw it were shocked and surprised. They asked the father lightling, "Who is this baby? Where did He come from?"

The father lightling answered, "He is not my son. He is the Son of the King of Light. The King has given Him to us as a special gift. He has been born for us. When He grows up, He will be called the Light of the World. There will be no darkness strong enough to hide His light, no darkness deep enough to send His light away."

When they heard this, the lightling children knelt down at the baby's feet and began to worship Him in fear and reverence.

When they stood up again, their own faces were shining. But the light that was shining in their faces was not coming from inside them; it was a reflection of the light coming out of the baby. The lightlings were now surrounded with the light of the child they had visited.

They rushed back to their homes, their friends, and their families as fast as their feet could carry them. When they got home, they were still shining. The other lightlings were frightened at the sight of them. They asked, "What happened to you?" So the lightling children told their story.

"We saw a baby who was shining with light. He is the Son of the King of Light. The King has given us a child. He has given us His own Son to be the Light of the World."

The lightlings noticed that already there was more light in the forest. Now they could begin to see where they were going. They could walk without falling. They could run and play without bumping into trees or rocks and getting bruised. Some still hid from the light, but others realized they didn't need to be afraid anymore. They saw that living in the light was much better than the darkness they were used to.

Grandpa looked at Charlie and said, "You see, Charlie, we're afraid of the dark because we were made to live in the light. But someday, all of us who love this Son will live with Him forever in heaven. When we go to the dwelling place of the Son, who is now the Light of the World, there will be no darkness at all. Not only that, there will be no moon. There won't be any stars or even a sun. There'll be no night lights, no lamps, no lanterns, not even any candles."

Charlie asked, "How can it be light there if there's no sun or lamps or candles? How can that be?"

His grandfather replied, "In the place where the King's Son now lives, the light that shines forever still comes from Him. He is the light in heaven. All who come into His presence will never be in darkness again."

"Wow," Charlie said, "that sure is a wonderful thing to look forward to."

And Grandpa replied, "Charlie, let me make a suggestion. Every time you see the sun, the moon, or the stars, or light a candle, or turn on your night light, remember the story of the child the King of Light brought into the darkness of this world. And remember that He gave us this baby as a present. As long as you remember that, you will never, ever have to be afraid of the darkness again."

About the Author

DR. R.C. SPROUL is the founder and chairman of Ligonier Ministries, an international Christian discipleship organization based near Orlando, Florida. He also serves as copastor at Saint Andrew's Chapel in Sanford, Florida, and as chancellor of Reformation Bible College. His teaching can be heard on the daily radio program *Renewing Your Mind*. He is the author of more than one hundred books, including *The Holiness of God* and several children's books, such as *The Donkey Who Carried a King*, *The Priest with Dirty Clothes*, and *The Prince's Poison Cup*. He also served as general editor of the *Reformation Study Bible*. Dr. Sproul and his wife, Vesta, make their home in Sanford, Florida.

About the Illustrator

JUSTIN GERARD is an illustrator living in northern Georgia. He has illustrated several children's books and numerous short stories published in elementary reading texts. His work has been featured in Spectrum Fantastic Arts, the Society of Illustrators, and the Illustrators Annual. He has a special love for good stories, tank strategy, and chocolate chip cookie dough. He is known for studying Renaissance and modern masters in an ongoing effort to distill their collective powers into a drink that he can sell for millions.

For Parents

We hope you and your child enjoyed reading *The Lightlings*. The following questions and Bible passages may be helpful to you in guiding your child into a deeper understanding of the scriptural truths behind *The Lightlings*.

1. Who is the real King of Light?

God is light, and in him is no darkness at all. — 1 JOHN 1:5b

2. Who are the real lightlings?

Then God said, "Let us make man in our image, after our likeness. . . ." So God created man in his own image, in the image of God he created him; male and female he created them. — GENESIS 1:26-27

3. The King made the lightlings to shine like Him. What was special about God's creation of people?

Then God said, "Let us make man in our image, after our likeness. And let them have dominion over the fish of the sea and over the birds of the heavens and over the livestock and over all the earth and over every creeping thing that creeps on the earth." So God created man in his own image, in the image of God he created him; male and female he created them. — GENESIS 1:26-27

When God created man, he made him in the likeness of God. — GENESIS 5:1

4. The lightlings disobeyed the King of Light. Have people ever done anything like that?

So when the woman saw that the tree was good for food, and that it was a delight to the eyes, and that the tree was to be desired to make one wise, she took of its fruit and ate, and she also gave some to her husband who was with her, and he ate. — GENESIS 3:6

5. When the lightlings disobeyed the King, they felt ashamed and ran from Him. What happened when people disobeyed God?

And they heard the sound of the LORD God walking in the garden in the cool of the day, and the man and his wife hid themselves from the presence of the LORD God among the trees of the garden. But the LORD God called to the man and said to him, "Where are you?" And he said, "I heard the sound of you in the garden, and I was afraid, because I was naked, and I hid myself." — GENESIS 3:8-10

– continued –

6. **When the lightlings left the garden, they soon found themselves in such deep darkness that they could see nothing and often hurt themselves. Do people who hate the true King of Light experience such misery?**

   We all once lived in the passions of our flesh, carrying out the desires of the body and the mind, and were by nature children of wrath, like the rest of mankind. — EPHESIANS 2:3

   For we ourselves were once foolish, disobedient, led astray, slaves to various passions and pleasures, passing our days in malice and envy, hated by others and hating one another. — TITUS 3:3

7. **Who is the real baby lightling who shined so brightly?**

   *Again Jesus spoke to them, saying, "I am the light of the world. Whoever follows me will not walk in darkness, but will have the light of life." —*JOHN 8:12

   "As long as I am in the world, I am the light of the world." — JOHN 9:5

8. **Some of the lightling children saw the light of the baby and sought him out. Who were some of the people who first sought out the real light of the world?**

   *Now after Jesus was born in Bethlehem of Judea in the days of Herod the king, behold, wise men from the east came to Jerusalem, saying, "Where is he who has been born king of the Jews? For we saw his star when it rose and have come to worship him." —*MATTHEW 2:1–2

   And in the same region there were shepherds out in the field, keeping watch over their flock by night. And an angel of the Lord appeared to them, and the glory of the Lord shone around them, and they were filled with fear. And the angel said to them, "Fear not, for behold, I bring you good news of a great joy that will be for all the people. For unto you is born this day in the city of David a Savior, who is Christ the Lord." . . . And suddenly there was with the angel a multitude of the heavenly host praising God and saying, "Glory to God in the highest, and on earth peace among those with whom he is pleased!" When the angels went away from them into heaven, the shepherds said to one another, "Let us go over to Bethlehem and see this thing that has happened, which the Lord has made known to us." And they went with haste and found Mary and Joseph, and the baby lying in a manger. — LUKE 2:8–16

   Now there was a man in Jerusalem, whose name was Simeon. . . . And it had been revealed to him by the Holy Spirit that he would not see death before he had seen the Lord's Christ. And he came in the Spirit into the temple, and when the parents brought in the child Jesus, . . . he took him up in his arms and blessed God and said, "Lord, now you are letting your servant depart in peace, according to your word; for my eyes have seen your salvation that you have prepared in the presence of all peoples, a light for revelation to the Gentiles, and for glory to your people Israel." — LUKE 2:25–32

   And there was a prophetess, Anna, the daughter of Phanuel, of the tribe of Asher. . . . She did not depart from the temple, worshiping with fasting and prayer night and day. And coming up at that very hour she began to give thanks to God and to speak of him to all who were waiting for the redemption of Jerusalem. — LUKE 2:36–38

9. **The baby lightling was the Son of the King of Light. Who was the Father of the real light of the world?**

> *All things have been handed over to me by my Father, and no one knows the Son except the Father, and no one knows the Father except the Son and anyone to whom the Son chooses to reveal him.* — MATTHEW 11:27

> *And the Holy Spirit descended on him in bodily form, like a dove; and a voice came from heaven, "You are my beloved Son; with you I am well pleased."* — LUKE 3:22

10. **After the lightling children worshiped the baby, their faces began to shine. What similar thing happens to those who worship the light of the world?**

> *And we all, with unveiled face, beholding the glory of the Lord, are being transformed into the same image from one degree of glory to another. For this comes from the Lord who is the Spirit.* — 2 CORINTHIANS 3:18

> *The new self . . . is being renewed in knowledge after the image of its creator.* — COLOSSIANS 3:10

11. **What did the lightling children do that those who meet the real light of the world should also do?**

> *"Go therefore and make disciples of all nations, baptizing them in the name of the Father and of the Son and of the Holy Spirit, teaching them to observe all that I have commanded you. And behold, I am with you always, to the end of the age."* — MATTHEW 28:19–20

> *But you will receive power when the Holy Spirit has come upon you, and you will be my witnesses in Jerusalem and in all Judea and Samaria, and to the end of the earth."* — ACTS 1:8

12. **Not all the lightlings wanted to go to the light. Do all people love the light of the world?**

> *And this is the judgment: the light has come into the world, and people loved the darkness rather than the light because their deeds were evil. For everyone who does wicked things hates the light and does not come to the light, lest his deeds should be exposed. But whoever does what is true comes to the light, so that it may be clearly seen that his deeds have been carried out in God.* — JOHN 3:19–21

> *For you are all children of light, children of the day. We are not of the night or of the darkness.* — 1 THESSALONIANS 5:5

13. **Grandpa tells Charlie that we are afraid of the dark because we were made to live in the light. Do you love the light of the world? Does loving him take away your fear of the dark?**

> *At one time you were darkness, but now you are light in the Lord. Walk as children of light.* — EPHESIANS 5:8

The Lightlings

Text: © 2006 by R.C. Sproul
Illustrations: © 2006 by Justin Gerard

Published by Reformation Trust Publishing
a division of Ligonier Ministries
421 Ligonier Court, Sanford, FL 32771
Ligonier.org   ReformationTrust.com

Printed in China
RR Donnelley
April 2017
First edition, eleventh printing

All rights reserved. No part of this publication may be reproduced, stored in a retrieval system, or transmitted in any form or by any means-electronic, mechanical, photocopy, recording, or otherwise-without the prior written permission of the publisher, Reformation Trust Publishing. The only exception is brief quotations in printed reviews.

Creative direction: Chris Larson
Cover and interior design: Chris Larson
Illustration: Justin Gerard

Scripture quotations are from the ESV® Bible (The Holy Bible, English Standard Version®), copyright © 2001 by Crossway, a publishing ministry of Good News Publishers. Used by permission. All rights reserved.

Library of Congress Cataloging-in-Publication Data

Sproul, R. C. (Robert Charles), 1939-
  The lightlings / written by R.C. Sproul; illustrated by Justin Gerard.
    p. cm.
  Summary: Charlie's fears of the dark are calmed by his grandfather's story of the Son of the King of Light brought into the world so that people need never fear the darkness.
  ISBN 1-56769-078-5
  [1. Fear of the dark--Fiction. 2. Christian life--Fiction.] I. Gerard, Justin, ill. II. Title.
  PZ7.S7693Lig 2006
  [E]--dc22
                    2006026301